Contents

Chapter One

Rose was getting ready for
school when Uncle Vinnie
walked in. He was working on a
building site nearby and often
dropped round for a cup of tea.

Rose was feeling grumpy. She didn't say hello to her uncle. She just pushed her books into her school bag and then dumped it on the kitchen table.

"What's up, Rose?" asked Uncle Vinnie.

Rose gave a big sigh. "I've got to talk about my book at school today, but I haven't read it. It's called *Sea Storm* and it's really hard. I wanted the book with an alien on the cover, but Zack Smith grabbed it. He's a bully and he always laughs when I stand up and talk in class."

"Hm." Uncle Vinnie sat down. He rubbed his chin and looked thoughtful. He was a very tall man with lots of white hair and a long nose. He was a builder but Rose thought he looked like a wizard.

"Bullies are usually scared of
something," said Uncle Vinnie.

"Not Zack," said Rose.

"Are you sure? Think hard."

Rose thought hard. She
thought of Zack pushing Lauren

Parks down the steps. She
thought of Zack throwing Ben
Wainwright's football over the
fence, and making Emma Bowler
give him her dinner money.

"Zack's not scared of anything," said Rose. "But everyone's scared of him."

"Think again. Perhaps there's something Zack doesn't like doing." Uncle Vinnie stared at Rose with his bright blue eyes; the sort of eyes that made you feel he could see right inside your head.

So Rose thought again. She thought of Zack jumping into the swimming pool, leaping off the climbing frame, tackling the bigger boys at football. Zack wasn't scared of anyone. And then she remembered something.

"He doesn't like stroking our classroom rat," she said.

"There you are then," said Uncle Vinnie.

"I don't see how that helps," said Rose.

Just then, Rose's mum called to her from the hall. "Come on, Rose. You'll miss the school bus."

Rose was about to run out when Uncle Vinnie said, "Wait!"

He took a small blue book out of his pocket. "I wasn't good at reading when I was at school," he said. "But I learned a trick."

"What sort of trick?" asked Rose.

"You tell them the story in this book." Uncle Vinnie popped the blue book into Rose's bag. "That's the trick."

"But I haven't read it!" argued Rose.

"That doesn't matter. As soon
as you open it, you'll know
what to say. It's about a rat and
it's — it's a kind of magic story.
It's about things we can't see.
Off you go now, and don't
worry!" Uncle Vinnie gave Rose
a big wink.

Chapter Two

Rose didn't have time to open
the book on the bus. Her friend,
Ben Wainwright, had saved her
a seat next to him, and he had
a lot to tell her about his dog
Jess and her twelve puppies.

When they got to school,
Rose and Ben walked through
the playground together. Zack
Smith was pushing Yusef Malik
against the railings. "Give me
those crisps or I'll thump you!"
he shouted.

Yusef handed over
his crisps. He looked as if he
was going to cry.

Ben said, "I wish we could do
something about Zack."

"Me too," said Rose. She told Ben about Uncle Vinnie. "My uncle says bullies are always scared of something, and I thought that maybe Zack was scared of Ratty. He never goes near the cage."

"Hey! I think you're right," said Ben.

They reached the classroom
and found that Lauren had taken
Ratty out of his cage. The white

rat was sitting
on her
shoulder and
some of
the other
children were
stroking him.
Zack came in and Rose noticed
that he wouldn't walk past
Lauren and the rat. He went
right round to the other side of
the classroom, and then came
back to his seat.

Zack shared a table with Rose, Ben and Lauren. He gave Rose a nasty look and said, "Have you read your book, then?"

"Yes," said Rose. She felt in her bag. Where was the blue book? Ah, there it was, under her trainers.

While Rose was trying to
tug the book out of her bag,
Mrs Feather, the teacher, came
in. She told Lauren to put
Ratty back in his cage and go
to her place.

Rose had just put the blue book on the table when Mrs Feather said, "Rose Ritchie, I want you to go first today. Tell us what your book is about."

Everyone looked at Rose. She opened the blue book.

There was nothing there. Nothing. No words. No pictures. She turned the pages. They were all blank. Every one. Blank. Rose stared at the empty pages. Her mouth dropped open. "Err . . ." she mumbled.

"Stand up, Rose. We can't hear you," said Mrs Feather.

Rose stood up. She felt
very hot. She knew her face
must be crimson.

"Well . . . we're waiting." Mrs Feather drummed her long nails on her desk. "Come on, Rose!" Zack leaned towards the blue book and Rose quickly picked it up. She didn't want him to see the blank pages. At that moment she noticed Ratty standing on his hind legs and looking at her with his red eyes.

"It's about a rat," said Rose.
"Yes. Go on, tell us some
more," said Mrs Feather.

"Well . . . er . . ." Rose didn't know what to say next. Uncle Vinnie said he'd learned a trick, but perhaps the trick was on her.

"Rose hasn't read her book. She can't read!" sang Zack.

"I *can*!" cried Rose. "It's just difficult to explain."

"Be quiet, Zack," said Mrs
Feather. "Let Rose think."

Rose thought. What had
Uncle Vinnie said? The book
was about things you couldn't
see. Invisible things.

Suddenly Rose knew what to say. "The story is about a rat that's invisible. His name is Vinnie and he's a very fierce rat. One day he gets out of his cage."

The class was very quiet. They were all looking at Rose. Zack had a scared expression on his face.

Rose told a story about a rat that had been made invisible by a wizard. The rat escaped from his cage and climbed into a boy's pocket. When the boy put his hand into his pocket, the rat chewed his finger off.

Zack frowned and looked at his fingers.

"And then Invisible Vinnie jumped out of the boy's pocket and ran into the woods where he had many strange and wonderful adventures," said Rose.

"Did he take the boy's finger with him?" asked Ben.

Rose glanced at Zack. He'd gone very white.

Chapter Three

At break Ben said to Rose, "It's true. Zack *is* afraid of rats. I saw his face when you were telling your rat story."

"I'm scared," said Rose. "I think he's going to get me. My

book didn't have any words in it. I made the story up."

"Did you?" Ben was surprised. "It was brilliant."

Rose saw Zack come into the playground with Pete Fowler and Russell Downs. When Zack saw Rose he walked over to her, followed by his gang.

"Where's that book?" Zack said. "The one about the invisible rat?"

"I haven't got it," said Rose.

"You have," snarled Zack. "I saw you put it in your pocket."

Ben said, "Leave her alone."

"Keep out of it," said Zack, and he gave Ben a shove that sent him tumbling to the ground.

Rose took off. She ran across the playground with Zack and his gang leaping after her. They were much faster than Rose. She didn't stand a chance.

Pete grabbed Rose's arm and
Zack pulled the book out of her
pocket.

"Aha!" cried Zack, opening
the book. "I thought so.
This book hasn't got any words
in it. You made them up, Rose
Ritchie. You can't read!"

"Rose can't read! Rose can't
read!" sang Pete and Russell.

Tears began to fill Rose's
eyes. And then she remembered
something Uncle Vinnie had said
– about things you can't see.

"I *can* read!" she cried. "A
wizard gave that book to me.
The words are invisible to *some*
people."

"Tah!" sneered Zack.

Mrs Feather was on duty in the playground. Zack went straight up to her and said, "Look at this book, Mrs Feather. It hasn't got any words in it. Rose made the story up."

Mrs Feather took the book
and opened it. "Oh!" she said.
"That's interesting. Come here,
Rose."

Rose walked across, dragging
her feet.

"Did you make your story up?"
asked Mrs Feather.

"No," mumbled Rose. "The words are invisible. I can read invisible writing."

Zack burst out laughing but Pete looked interested. Mrs Feather didn't laugh. She said, "I see," and gave the book back to Rose. The bell went for the end of break and everyone ran indoors.

Ben was already sitting at
the table when Rose went
into the classroom. He had a
funny look on his face.

"Did Zack hurt you?" asked
Rose.

"Nah!" said Ben.

Lauren came and sat beside Rose. "I saw what Zack did to you both in break," she said.

Ben leaned towards them and whispered, "Well, I'm going to teach him a lesson."

Zack marched over and sat at the table. He pushed Lauren's crayons out of the way and they rolled onto the floor. Her favourite blue crayon broke into bits. "Nooo!" she cried.

"You're too messy, Lauren,"
said Zack. "You take up too
much space."

Lauren put the broken crayon
on the table, but she didn't say
anything.

Rose caught Lauren's eye, and they both looked at Ben, who was grinning.

What was Ben going to do? How could he teach Zack a lesson?

Chapter Four

Ben usually played football
in the dinner break. Today he
just stood by the railings,
looking anxious.

Rose and Lauren went over to him. "What's up, Ben?" said Rose. "Don't you feel well?"

"I'm fine," he said. "But I'm going to go back to the classroom and hide Ratty."

Lauren gasped.

"Shh! I don't want anyone to know," Ben whispered.

"What are you going to do with him?" asked Rose.

"I'm going to put him in my pencil tin then, just before the end of school, I'll tell Mrs Feather he doesn't seem to be in his cage."

"She'll make us look for him."

"But I'll make sure he isn't found," said Ben, "and we'll watch Zack. I bet he's scared."

"Brilliant!" said Lauren.

Ben went back to the classroom five minutes early. He put all his pens and pencils on the table and carefully lifted Ratty into the tin. It was a very large tin and Ben had dropped it so many times the lid didn't fit properly, so Ratty would get plenty of air.

Ben put some torn paper and a biscuit beside the rat, to keep him happy. He was just closing the lid when Zack walked in.

"Why's your stuff all over the table?" Zack asked Ben.

"I can't get it in my tin," said Ben. He put the tin under his chair, out of harm's way. Zack looked suspicious. He would probably have pushed all Ben's stuff off the table if Mrs Feather hadn't come in.

The classroom was very noisy just before the first lesson, so no one heard Ratty chewing his biscuit. But then the noise died down and Mrs Feather began to talk.

A faint scratching sound could be heard. It seemed to be coming from under Ben's chair. Ben coughed to cover the noise.

Ratty was quiet for a few minutes, and then he started scratching again, so Lauren sneezed.

Next time Ratty made a noise, Rose pretended to get hiccups.

"What's the matter with you three?" asked Mrs Feather.

Ben, Rose and Lauren were silent. Suddenly, Ratty started rustling the paper. Ben coughed, Lauren sneezed and Rose hiccuped.

"What's going on?" said Mrs Feather suspiciously.

Ben realized he couldn't keep coughing all through the lesson, so he said, "Ratty doesn't seem to be in his cage, Mrs Feather."

Everyone looked at the cage.

"Goodness," said Mrs Feather. She opened the cage door and felt under the straw. "Oh dear, he's escaped," she said. "Quickly, everyone on the floor. Look under the tables. We mustn't let him get into the corridor."

Everyone dropped to their knees. Everyone except Zack.

He sat on his chair with his
knees pulled up to his chin.

"I see him!" cried Ben.

"He's under your chair, Zack!"

"Oh yes. There he is," said Rose.

Zack leapt off the chair and
ran across the room.

"He's coming your way,
Zack!" cried Lauren.

"No! No!" cried Zack.

"Calm down, Zack," said
Mrs Feather.

"You're not afraid of rats, are
you?" said Rose.

"No!" screamed Zack.

"He's right by your foot," said Ben.

"I don't see him," said Mrs Feather.

"He's invisible," said Rose. "Just like Vinnie. Ooo – now he's on your shoe, Zack!"

"AAAAAH!" shrieked Zack.
He jumped up on a table, white
with terror.

Pete was the first one to laugh, and then Russell joined in. Zack's gang was laughing at him, and very soon everyone else was laughing too.

With a terrible cry, Zack jumped off the table and ran out of the room.

"Zack, come back!" said Mrs Feather, chasing him down the corridor.

While she was gone, Ben sneaked Ratty back into his cage. "Don't tell," he said to the rest of the class. "Promise you won't tell?"

"Course we won't tell," said Pete. "That was the best joke ever."

Lauren leaned over to Rose. "I reckon Zack's lost his gang," she whispered.

Chapter Five

A few minutes later Mrs Feather
came back with Zack.

"I found Ratty," Ben told her.
"He's back in his cage."

"Well done, Ben," said Mrs Feather.

Zack shuffled back to his table. His eyes were red and he wouldn't look at anyone. He was completely silent for the rest of the day. It made a nice change. As soon as the bell rang Zack went up to Mrs Feather's desk and gave her something out of his bag. Then he looked at Rose and left the room.

Mrs Feather called Rose over to her desk. Rose was worried. She thought she was going to be told off.

"I'll wait for you outside," said Ben.

But Mrs Feather didn't tell Rose off. She said, "Zack thinks you might like to read this." She held out the book with an alien on the cover. "So we'll swap it for *Sea Storm*, shall we?"

"Yes, *please!*" said Rose. She ran and got *Sea Storm* out of her bag.

Mrs. Feather gave her the alien book.

"Thanks, Mrs Feather," said Rose.

"Don't thank me, thank Zack," said Mrs Feather.

"Oh," said Rose thoughtfully. 'OK."

She was about to go when
Mrs Feather said, "By the
way, that was a very good
story you told about Invisible
Vinnie. D'you think you
could make up another one and
write it down?"

"Of course," said Rose
beaming.

★

When Rose got home Uncle
Vinnie was sitting in the kitchen
with Rose's mum, having a cup
of tea.

"Well, you look more
cheerful, Rose," said her mum.
"How did you get on with
the book?" asked Uncle Vinnie.

"Brilliantly!" said Rose. And she told her mum and her uncle the story of Invisible Vinnie.

Uncle Vinnie shook his wild wizard's hair and laughed till he cried.

"You played a trick on me,"
said Rose sternly, "but I forgive
you, because it worked like
magic."

THE END